Once upon a time there lived a wise and wealthy King. But the King was sad for he had no children. Then one day, to King William's joy, the baby princess Odette was born. Kings and Queens came from far and wide to greet the new Princess. Queen Uberta came with her small son, Derek. She watched proudly while Derek gave the new baby a pretty little locket.

At that moment both Queen Uberta and King William had a wonderful idea. The two children might grow up to fall in love with one another. Then they could marry and unite the two great kingdoms of King William and Queen Uberta.

Rothbart, an evil enchanter, was greedily plotting against the King and Queen. With the power of magic potions and spells, Rothbart planned to take the two kingdoms of King William and Queen Uberta and have them for himself.

On the very night of the plot, Rothbart was discovered. King William, in a rage, destroyed the wicked enchanter's hiding place and banished him from the kingdom.

"I'm not finished yet," vowed Rothbart. One day he would return to seek revenge.

The two young children met every summer just as Queen Uberta and King William had planned. But Odette and Derek were shy and awkward. They refused to play together. They teased each other. They did not seem to like each other at all. Each summer they disliked each other more and more until the King and Queen had almost given up hope that Derek and Odette would ever marry.

$\mathfrak{N}$ow Odette was growing into a beautiful young woman. Derek had grown tall and handsome. One summer, when Odette arrived for her visit, Derek's heart missed a beat when he first saw her as they met in the ballroom. He could hardly believe that she was the same girl. Derek could think of nothing but Odette. All that wonderful summer, Derek and Odette talked and dreamed together. They were very happy.

King William and Queen Uberta were delighted.

$\mathcal{A}$t the royal ball, as Odette and Derek danced happily together, Derek suddenly announced loudly to everyone that the wedding could be arranged. "Wait!" cried Odette. The dancing stopped.

"But why?" pleaded Derek. "You're all I've ever wanted. You're beautiful."

Odette was dismayed. "But what else?" she asked. "Is beauty all that matters to you?"

"What else is there?" Derek asked foolishly.

He did not understand that Odette wanted him to say that he loved her. Odette sadly left the ballroom. She was sure that after all Derek did not love her. The marriage would not take place.

$\mathcal{T}$he next day King William and Princess Odette set out for their own kingdom. Deep into the forest went the royal carriage.

Suddenly the way was blocked by a dark figure. The carriage stopped and King William got out. Then he recognised the cloaked figure. It was Rothbart.

In an instant there was a fireball of light and the evil enchanter was transformed into a terrifying animal. The hideous monster attacked with a deafening roar.

King William's Captain managed to escape and brought news of the attack by a Great Animal. Derek was horrified. He raced for his horse and galloped through the rain far into the forest, searching for Odette's carriage. There he found only broken wheels and splintered wood. In the wreckage lay King William.

"Who has done this?" cried Derek. "Where is Odette?"

"It's not what it seems," whispered the King. "Odette has gone."

"Odette!" Derek cried out in sorrow for his lost love.

$\mathcal{A}$ lonely swan glided sadly on a lake below a dark castle. Rothbart, the evil enchanter, watched the beautiful bird.

"My spell will not last the whole day, Odette," laughed Rothbart. "Every night, when the moon comes up, when the light touches your wings, you will change back into the Princess." As Rothbart spoke, the moonlight touched the swan and she was changed back into Princess Odette. Rothbart warned Odette that she had to be on the lake for the magic to work. As soon as the moonlight left the lake she would become a swan once more.

"The spell will not be broken unless you marry me," gloated Rothbart, "or unless you find someone who will declare everlasting love to you and prove it to the world."

Odette was in despair. How could she ever leave the lake?

"Poor Odette," groaned Jean-Bob the frog and Speed the turtle, as they watched Odette turn from swan to princess and back to swan again as the days passed. Jean-Bob loved Princess Odette and he and Speed became her best friends.

One day Odette rescued a wounded puffin. Lieutenant Puffin was a brave and clever bird and when he saw what had happened to Odette he thought of a plan to break the spell.

"We will find Derek and bring him back to the lake, just as the moon is coming up," said Puffin. "When he sees the swan change into Princess Odette everyone will be happy ever after!"

$\mathcal{D}$erek had also been making plans. He was sure that Odette was still alive and he wanted to hunt for the Great Animal and find Odette. He needed to practise some archery to make himself ready to rescue the Princess.

Bromley, Derek's friend, trembled as Lord Rogers tied an apple on his head. Derek was about to try Catch and Fire.

"Oh please, oh please, oh please," squeaked Bromley. He had to fire his own arrow at Derek. The arrow flew through the air. Derek spun round and caught it. Then with one move Derek loaded his own bow with the arrow and fired it back. Bromley closed his eyes and the arrow split the apple right in two.

Derek was pleased. Now he was ready to find Odette.

What was the Great Animal? Derek searched through the royal library. Perhaps he would find the answer in a book.

"It's not what it seems," he thought.

What had King William tried to say?

He turned over the dusty pages of a huge, old book. Suddenly he stopped.

There was the answer.

"I'm going to find the Great Animal," shouted Derek to his mother as he raced past her.

"But the royal ball is tomorrow night. You must be there," cried Queen Uberta.

"I'll try to be back in time," called Derek.

Even as Derek was showing Bromley how a tiny mouse could change into a terrible monster, Odette and Puffin were flying through the forest searching for Derek.

"We're looking for an animal that can change its shape," Derek explained to Bromley. "A harmless creature approaches and suddenly . . ."

Derek stopped. He was listening. "I'm sure it's here Bromley."

Suddenly a golden light flashed above the treetops.

Derek raised his bow and arrow and saw to his amazement a beautiful white bird flying down towards him.

"A swan!" cried Derek. "Of course! It's not what it seems."

This must be the Great Animal! As the swan flew closer, Derek aimed his arrow. It sped through the air straight to the swan.

Puffin dived out of the sky and knocked Odette out of the path of the arrow. They both flew off in fright with Derek running after them through the forest below.

"It's working," cried Puffin. "Look, here he comes."

Odette was very frightened. Derek had not recognised her, but how could he when she was a swan. Why did he want to hurt her? She must get back to the lake.

"Fly into the sun, Odette," called Puffin. "Follow me."

Puffin and Odette flew though the trees and soared up into the sky while Derek shielded his eyes from the sun, as he raced on after them through the forest.

The sun had set and the moonlight was creeping over the lake as Derek came out of the forest and onto the shore of the lake. He stood in amazement as the swan swooped down to the water in front of him.

"Be brave, Odette," called Puffin, as Derek raised his bow again. The moonlight came closer and closer and Derek took aim.

$\mathcal{A}$ magical light swirled and sparkled around the swan. Derek watched in awe as the swan changed into the Princess Odette.

"Hello, Derek," Odette said quietly.

As they ran joyfully into each others arms, Derek's bow fell to the ground.

"Oh, Odette, I knew you were alive," cried Derek.

"You cannot stay," warned Odette, as a thunderous voice from the castle called her name. "I am under a spell and when the moon sets I will be changed back into a swan."

"How can the spell be broken?" asked Derek.

"You must make a vow of eternal love and prove it to the world."

Derek remembered the royal ball the next night. Odette must go to the palace. There he would swear his love for her to everyone at the ball. Odette was overjoyed.

$\mathcal{A}$s Rothbart roared again for Odette, Derek kissed her and sped away into the forest.

"Didn't you hear me calling?" shouted Rothbart. "I thought I heard voices."

In his hand he held the bow which Derek had dropped.

"You will never go to the ball," he said. "You cannot fool me."

Odette grew numb as Rothbart threw the bow into the lake.

"You cannot stop me," cried Odette.

But Rothbart smiled nastily at her. "You have forgotten one thing," he said. "There will be no moon tomorrow night."

Rothbart and his Hag cackled with laughter as he told her how Derek had seen Odette. Then Rothbart grew silent as he realised that Derek's vow could still break the spell. What could he do to stop him? He eyed the old woman in front of him.

"I'll get Derek to offer his vow of love at the ball to the wrong princess," he cried. "I'll make you look like Princess Odette! You will go to the ball instead."

Odette was locked in the water dungeon of Rothbart's castle.

"What a shame you can't go to the ball," he jeered down at her, "but this poor fellow who got lost in the woods can keep you company instead."

Then Bromley was pushed roughly through a door of the tower and tumbled down into the water.

"Help!" shouted Bromley. "I can't swim."

Odette held onto him and pulled him to safety. Rothbart laughed cruelly and slammed the dungeon door shut.

$\mathcal{A}$t the royal palace the ballroom was filled with beautiful princesses, all longing to dance with the handsome Prince Derek. Queen Uberta felt delighted and was quite sure that Derek would choose a princess to marry.

But Derek had a secret. He was waiting for Odette to arrive. Oh, where was she?

Suddenly there was a loud knocking at the ballroom door. The door opened and there was a hushed silence as a beautiful princess walked down the stairs. Derek gazed at her in joy.

"Odette," he said to himself. "This time I won't let you leave."

hile Prince Derek danced with his dream princess, the real Princess Odette was still a prisoner in the water dungeon. Puffin, Jean-Bob and Speed were determined to help her escape.

"There must be a hole in the dungeon wall," said Puffin. "We'll find it and make it big enough for Odette to escape through."

"Don't forget the alligators," said Jean-Bob.

While Speed and Puffin dug at the dungeon wall, the alligators chased poor Jean-Bob until at last the hole was ready.

"To the rescue, mademoiselle," cried Jean-Bob. Odette dived down through the hole and shot up through the water and into the sky. She was free!

erek should have been happy now he was with his princess. Yet he felt that something was not right.

"Odette," he said, "you seem different somehow."

The princess did not reply, but showed him the locket that Derek had given Odette when she was a little baby.

Derek felt better. Here was Odette. Now was the time to make his vow of eternal love.

"I have an announcement to make," he called to everyone in the ballroom.

All this time the true Odette was flying as fast as she could to the palace.

Above the ballroom Odette beat at the window with her wings. She could see Derek below, holding the hand of a princess.

"Today I have found my bride," he was saying.

"No, Derek! It's a trick," cried Odette. But Derek could not hear her desperate cries.

"Before the world I make a vow stronger than all the powers on earth," said Derek, smiling at the princess. Odette beat her wings in vain at the closed windows as Derek made his vow.

". . . a vow of everlasting love to Odette."

Suddenly the windows of the ballroom crashed open and an icy cold wind whipped through the room. There stood Rothbart.

"You've pledged your love to another," he mocked Derek. "Odette is mine."

Rothbart raised his arm over the princess and in a blazing light, she fell to the ground. There in her place lay the ugly, old Hag.

"Where is Odette?" cried Prince Derek.

"She will die," said Rothbart. "Look!"

A white swan was flying slowly away above the palace.

Odette flew slower and slower across the tree tops and down to the lake. She could barely lift her wings. She plunged down, down onto the stones by the lake and lay still.

Jean-Bob, Speed and Puffin gathered round her. "Please don't die," wept Jean-Bob.

As he spoke, a light shone around the body of the swan. When it faded away there was Princess Odette, lying on the stones.

She did not move.

When Derek had seen the swan flying away above him, he had raced from the palace and through the forest calling Odette's name. At the lake he found her and knelt by her side.

"It's you I love. The vow I made was for you," Derek cried as he held her in his arms. He looked up to see Rothbart watching him.

"Don't you dare let her die," shouted Derek. "You have the power to save her!"

"Only if you defeat me," snarled a terrible voice. Rothbart had turned into the Great Animal. It was ready to attack.

The Great Animal was powerful and cruel. It grabbed at Prince Derek with its talons and hurled him to the ground.

"The bow," shouted Puffin. "Swim to bottom of the lake and get the Prince's bow."

Jean-Bob dived down into the water to find the bow. Speed came too and together they pulled up the bow and threw it to the Prince as he lay on the ground.

The Great Animal was racing down out of the sky. Derek reached for the bow, but there were no arrows.

"Oh please, oh please," called a familiar voice. It was Bromley.

He had escaped from the dungeon and was ready to fire an arrow from his bow for Derek. The arrow flew towards the Prince. He spun round, caught the arrow in mid-air and fitted it into his own bow. The Great Animal swooped down and Derek fired the arrow straight into his heart.

With a great cry the Animal fell into the lake.

Once more Prince Derek held Princess Odette in his arms.

"Forgive me, Odette," he begged. "I only wanted to prove my love for you."

Slowly the Princess opened her eyes. "Oh Derek," she whispered.

They embraced each other and the colour returned to Odette's pale cheeks.

Derek had made his vow of everlasting love.

Now Odette knew that they would live happily ever after.

the Swan princess™

from the story by Richard Rich and Brian Nissen

and the film by Richard Rich

First published in Great Britain in 1995 by Mammoth
an imprint of Reed Children's Books
Michelin House, 81 Fulham Road, London SW3 6RB
and Auckland, Melbourne, Singapore and Toronto

Line illustrations by Emilie Kong Studios
Copyright © 1994 by Nest Productions, Inc.

ISBN 0 7497 2027 1

A CIP catalogue record for this title is available from the British Library

Printed in Great Britain
by Cambus Litho Ltd.